Fun
Picnic

Om
KIDZ
An imprint of Om Books International

Om KIDZ | Om Books International

Reprinted in 2018

Corporate & Editorial Office
A-12, Sector 64, Noida 201 301
Uttar Pradesh, India
Phone: +91 120 477 4100
Email: editorial@ombooks.com
Website: www.ombooksinternational.com

© Om Books International 2017

ISBN: 978-93-86108-37-1

Printed in India

10 9 8 7 6 5 4 3 2

Sales Office
107, Ansari Road, Darya Ganj
New Delhi 110 002, India
Phone: +91 11 4000 9000
Email: sales@ombooks.com
Website: www.ombooks.com

Fun at the Picnic

I'm all set to read

Paste your photograph here

My name is
_____

It is Sunday. **The Sun** is up in **the sky**. **Sam** is going **for** a picnic with **his mom**, **dad and** little sister **Sue**.

Mom brings a **big** picnic basket. **Dad** carries a **mat**. **Sam** carries **his bat and** ball. Baby **Sue** carries **her** soft **toy cat**! **All** of them **get** into **the car**.

"**Let** us go!" says **Dad**.

Mom drives the car. They go out of the city. Sam sees green fields. "Cow!" says Sue, pointing outside. A big, fat cow is grazing on the fields.

They reach **the** picnic spot. It is next to a **dam**.

"**Let** us **sit** here!" says **Sam**. He points to a shaded spot below a **big oak** tree. **Dad** places **the mat** below **the** tree.

Sam holds up **his bat**. "**Let** us have some **fun**!" he says.

Dad throws a ball. **Sam** hits it with **his bat**. **The** ball flies **far** into **the** grass. "Oh no, we lost it!" cries **Sam**.

Just then, something moves in **the** grass. A furry, brown **dog** comes running **out**. He is holding **the** ball in **his** mouth.

The dog comes to Sam. It gives him the ball. Then, it holds out its paw. "Look, the dog is saying hello!" says Sam.

The dog joins their game **too**.
After some time, they feel hungry.
Mom opens **the** basket. **She** pulls
out a **big box** of **jam** sandwiches.

They **all eat the jam** sandwiches. **Mom** gives them a **cup** of orange juice each.

It's getting **hot**. **Sue** plays with **her toy cat**. **Sam** sits on **the mat and** plays with **the dog**. He wants to take **the dog** home.

"**Mom**, **Dad**, **can** we take **the dog** home?" asks **Sam**.

"I do **not** think that's a good idea," says **Mom**. "He is someone else's **dog**."

"**Can** we please **get** a **dog**?"
asks **Sam**.

"**Dog!**" says **Sue**.

Mom and Dad laugh. "We will **get
one for** your birthday!" they **say**.

Sam and Sue are so happy! This is **the** best picnic they've ever **had**.

Find and circle three-letter words in the grid below.

R	Z	B	P	L
O	M	A	T	C
D	O	G	H	A
M	G	H	E	R
W	H	X	V	E

Match these words to the correct pictures.

DOG •

CAT •

BAT •

BOX •

COW •

Unscramble the letters on the mat to make some three-letter words!

JMA   ATC   HMI

___   ___   ___

EHT   TYO   GDO

___   ___   ___

ONT   TEG

___   ___

Know your words

Sight Words

the	all	out	not
for	get	too	one
his	let	hot	are
and	out	him	had
big	fat	its	
her	far	she	

Naming Words

Sam	Dad	can	paw
Sue	mat	cow	box
sun	bat	dam	jam
sky	toy	oak	cup
Mom	cat	dog	car

Doing Words

sit	eat	say